BABASAH

RAMJI SAKPAL OF AMBADVE* WHO WAS A SUBEDAR IN THE ARMY, WAS STATIONED AT MHOW. ONE OF HIS UNCLES WHO WAS AN ASCETIC, HAPPENED TO BE IN MHOW ONE DAY, AND RAMJI CHANCED TO MEET HIM.

DO US THE HONOUR OF VISITING OUR HOME, UNCLE.
I HAVE RENOUNCED THE WORLD. I CANNOT COME.

THE SANYASI WAS TOUCHED BY RAMJI'S DISAPPOINTED FACE.
NEVERTHELESS, I BLESS YOU. YOU SHALL HAVE A SON, WHO WILL ACHIEVE WORLD-WIDE FAME.

* IN RATNAGIRI DISTRICT.

ON APRIL 14, 1891, RAMJI'S WIFE, BHIMABAI, GAVE BIRTH TO A SON.
LET'S CALL HIM BHIM— A NAME BEFITTING ONE DESTINED TO BE GREAT. WE WILL GIVE HIM EVERYTHING HE NEEDS, EVEN IF WE HAVE TO STARVE.
I AM A SUBEDAR-MAJOR NOW. WE DON'T HAVE TO STARVE TO GIVE HIM A GOOD EDUCATION.

TWO YEARS LATER, RAMJI RETIRED FROM THE ARMY AND MOVED WITH HIS FAMILY TO DAPOLI IN THE KONKAN. BHIM WAS ENROLLED IN SCHOOL WHEN HE WAS FIVE YEARS OLD.
HOW CAN WE AFFORD TO EDUCATE BHIM ON THE SMALL PENSION YOU GET?
DON'T WORRY! ALL WILL BE WELL. SOME FRIENDS HAVE PROMISED TO HELP ME TO FIND A JOB.

RAMJI SOON GOT A JOB IN SATARA AND THEIR HOPES ROSE AGAIN. BUT TRAGEDY STRUCK THE FAMILY. BHIMABAI, WHO HAD BEEN AILING, DIED.
WHO WILL LOOK AFTER MY MOTHERLESS CHILDREN?
BROTHER, DO NOT WORRY. I WILL LOOK AFTER THEM, AND LITTLE BHIM SHALL HAVE MY SPECIAL ATTENTION.
SO RAMJI'S SISTER, MIRA, TOOK CHARGE OF THE CHILDREN.

RAMJI, WHO WAS A TRAINED TEACHER, LOOKED AFTER THE EDUCATION OF HIS SONS.

HE ALSO READ STORIES FROM THE MAHABHARATA AND RAMAYANA AND SANG DEVOTIONAL SONGS TO HIS FAMILY.

WHEN BHIM COMPLETED HIS PRIMARY EDUCATION, HE WAS ADMITTED TO HIGH SCHOOL. HE WAS MADE TO SIT IN A CORNER OF THE CLASS, SEGREGATED FROM THE OTHER STUDENTS.
BHIMRAO AMBADVEKAR!
PRESENT, SIR.

WHEN THE RECESS BELL RANG, ALL THE BOYS RAN OUT TO PLAY AND TO DRINK WATER. BHIM, WHO WAS THIRSTY TOO, REACHED FOR THE CUP—
ARRE! DON'T TOUCH THAT!

HOLD OUT YOUR HANDS. I'LL POUR OUT SOME WATER FOR YOU.

BHIM HELD OUT HIS CUPPED PALMS OBEDIENTLY BUT HE WAS HURT.
WHAT IS WRONG WITH ME? WHY SHOULD I BE TREATED DIFFERENTLY?

ONCE BHIM AND HIS ELDER BROTHER HAD TO TRAVEL TO KOREGAON, WHERE RAMJI WORKED AS A CASHIER. THEY GOT DOWN AT MASUR STATION AND WAITED FOR THEIR FATHER.
WHY HASN'T BABA COME?

AFTER WAITING FOR A LONG TIME, THEY HIRED A BULLOCK-CART WITH THE HELP OF THE STATION MASTER.
WHOSE CHILDREN ARE YOU?
WE ARE RAMJI SAKPAL'S CHILDREN. WE'RE ON OUR WAY TO MEET HIM.

RAMJI SAKPAL? GET OFF MY CART, YOU UNTOUCH-ABLES!
PLEASE, DON'T THROW US OUT!

TAKE PITY ON US, PLEASE! WE DON'T KNOW HOW TO GET TO KOREGAON. WE'LL BE STRANDED.

I AM POLLUTED, MY CART IS POLLUT-ED, MY BULLOCKS ARE POLLUTED!
WE'LL PAY DOUBLE FARE. PLEASE TAKE US TO KOREGAON.
WE ARE WELL-DRESSED AND CLEAN. HOW CAN THE CART BE POLLUTED BY OUR TOUCH?

THE CARTMAN'S GREED GOT THE BETTER OF HIS HORROR OF POLLUTION.
ALL RIGHT! ALL RIGHT! YOU DRIVE THE CART. I'LL WALK BEHIND. I CAN PURIFY THE CART LATER.

ALL THROUGH THE JOURNEY, BHIM BROODED OVER THE INCIDENT.
WE ARE HUMAN BEINGS. YET THEY SAY OUR TOUCH DEFILES EVEN ANIMALS AND LIFELESS CARTS. WHY?

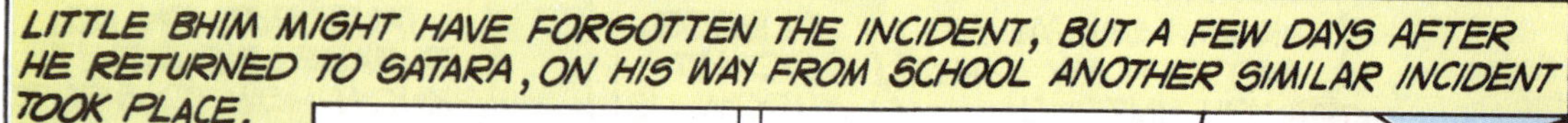
LITTLE BHIM MIGHT HAVE FORGOTTEN THE INCIDENT, BUT A FEW DAYS AFTER HE RETURNED TO SATARA, ON HIS WAY FROM SCHOOL ANOTHER SIMILAR INCIDENT TOOK PLACE.

MY THROAT IS PARCHED. I'LL DRAW SOME WATER FROM THAT WELL.

HEY, LOOK AT THAT UNTOUCHABLE!
HE HAS POLLUTED OUR WATER!

THE NEXT MOMENT—
LEAVE ME ALONE! WHAT WRONG HAVE I DONE?
YOU WRETCH! HOW DARE YOU TALK BACK!

BHIM WEPT BITTERLY.

AS HE GREW UP, SUCH INSULTS WERE EXPERIENCED MORE FREQUENTLY.
BHIM, YOUR HAIR NEEDS CUTTING. LET ME DO IT FOR YOU.
WHY CAN'T I GO TO A BARBER LIKE THE OTHER BOYS IN MY SCHOOL?

TEARS FILLED HIS SISTER'S EYES.
WE ARE MAHARS, UNTOUCHABLES.
BUT WHY? WHAT MAKES US DIFFERENT?

I DON'T KNOW. THAT'S THE WAY IT HAS ALWAYS BEEN.
BHIM WAS NOT SATISFIED WITH HIS SISTER'S REPLY.

BHIM FOUND AN OASIS OF WARM AFFECTION FOR HIM IN HIS BRAHMAN TEACHER, AMBEDKAR.
HE IS THE ONLY ONE WHO WILL LET ME COME NEAR HIM.
GOOD! YOU HAVE DONE ALL THE SUMS CORRECTLY.

DURING THE LUNCH BREAK—
COME ON, BHIM, EAT WITH ME.
BUT SIR....

WON'T YOU KEEP YOUR TEACHER COMPANY? COME, LET'S EAT.

ONCE WHILE THE TWO OF THEM WERE HAVING LUNCH TOGETHER—
BHIM, I AM GOING TO CHANGE YOUR SURNAME FROM AMBADVEKAR TO AMBEDKAR.
AS YOU WISH, SIR.

ONE NIGHT, MIRA CALLED THE THREE BOYS TO HER.
CHILDREN, YOU WILL HAVE A NEW MOTHER SOON, YOUR FATHER HAS DECIDED TO MARRY AGAIN.
OH, NO!

SHE WILL WEAR MY MOTHER'S ORNAMENTS AND RUN HER KITCHEN. NO! NEVER! I CAN'T STAY HERE.

I WILL RUN AWAY TO BOMBAY AND GET A JOB THERE. BUT HOW CAN I RAISE THE MONEY FOR THE FARE? I'LL STEAL AUNTY'S PURSE.

THREE NIGHTS HE TRIED WITHOUT SUCCESS. ON THE FOURTH NIGHT—
AH! I'VE GOT IT AT LAST!

HE EAGERLY OPENED THE PURSE —
WHAT ! ONLY ONE SMALL COIN ! MY POOR AUNT ! AND I WAS GOING TO ROB HER OF THIS !

BHIM PUT THE PURSE WITH THE MONEY BACK, AND WENT TO BED.
GOD ! FORGIVE ME FOR MY SIN. I SHALL MEND MY WAYS. I'LL STUDY HARD AND MAKE HER HAPPY WHEN I GROW UP.

BHIM PUT HIS HEART AND SOUL INTO HIS STUDIES AND WON THE ADMIRATION OF HIS TEACHERS.
RAMJI, YOUR SON IS VERY INTELLIGENT. HE DESERVES THE BEST POSSIBLE EDUCATION.
I'LL TRY, TO GIVE IT TO HIM, SIR.

RAMJI MOVED WITH HIS CHILDREN TO BOMBAY. HE TOOK UP A ROOM IN A CHAWL IN THE MILL AREA AT PAREL. THE ROOM SERVED AS KITCHEN, BEDROOM AND STUDY.
BHIM, YOU CAN'T STUDY IN ALL THIS NOISE. GO TO BED NOW. I'LL WAKE YOU UP AT TWO IN THE MORNING.
ALL RIGHT, FATHER.

AND BHIM SLEPT ON THE FLOOR.

AT TWO IN THE MORNING—
BHIM, IT'S TIME TO GET UP.

BHIM STUDIED WHILE THE OTHERS SLEPT.

ONE DAY AT ELPHINSTONE HIGH SCHOOL, IN BOMBAY—
BHIM, COME TO THE BLACK-BOARD.

* RAO IS AN HONORIFIC, USED IN MAHARASHTRA.

AFTER THE MEETING—
RAMJI, WHAT DO YOU PROPOSE NEXT FOR YOUR BRILLIANT SON?
HIS MARRIAGE WILL HAVE TO BE ARRANGED FIRST, KELUSKAR SAHEB.
EARLY MARRIAGE WAS COMMON IN THOSE DAYS.

BUT WHAT ABOUT HIS EDUCATION?
OF COURSE I WILL EDUCATE HIM, NO MATTER WHAT IT COSTS.

BHIM WAS MARRIED TO RAMABAI.

RAMJI CONTINUED TO PAY FOR HIS EDUCATION, EVEN THOUGH IT PUT A GREAT STRAIN ON HIS RESOURCES. BUT WHEN BHIM PASSED THE INTERMEDIATE ARTS EXAMINATION—
FATHER, YOU HAVE NOT YET GIVEN ME MY COLLEGE FEES.

SON, I HAVE NO MONEY.
WHAT SHALL I DO, FATHER? THE COLLEGE HAS WARNED ME ABOUT IT TWICE ALREADY AND I DON'T WANT TO GO TODAY WITHOUT THE FEES.

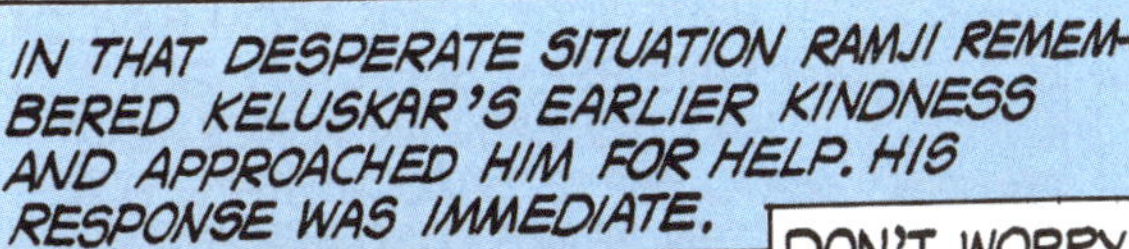
IN THAT DESPERATE SITUATION RAMJI REMEMBERED KELUSKAR'S EARLIER KINDNESS AND APPROACHED HIM FOR HELP. HIS RESPONSE WAS IMMEDIATE.

DON'T WORRY, RAMJI. I'LL TAKE BHIMRAO TO MAHARAJA SAYAJI RAO GAEKWAD OF BARODA. I AM SURE, HE WILL HELP.

AND SOON—
FATHER, MAHARAJA GAEKWAD HAS GRANTED ME A MONTHLY SCHOLARSHIP OF TWENTY-FIVE RUPEES. YOU WON'T NEED TO WORRY ANY MORE.
VERY GOOD. I MUST GO AND THANK SHRI KELUSKAR.

BHIM PASSED HIS B.A. IN 1912.
I HAVE BEEN GIVEN A JOB IN THE BARODA STATE SERVICES, BUT THE SALARY IS MEAGRE.

BHIM WENT TO BARODA. BARELY FIFTEEN DAYS LATER, BAD NEWS REACHED HIM—
"BABA SERIOUSLY ILL. COME AT ONCE."

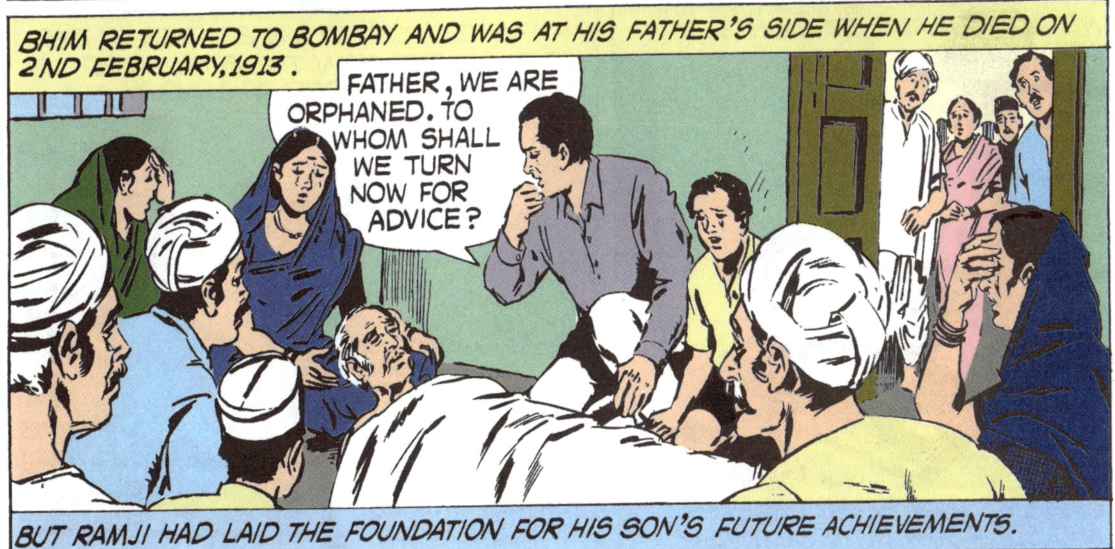
BHIM RETURNED TO BOMBAY AND WAS AT HIS FATHER'S SIDE WHEN HE DIED ON 2ND FEBRUARY, 1913.
FATHER, WE ARE ORPHANED. TO WHOM SHALL WE TURN NOW FOR ADVICE?
BUT RAMJI HAD LAID THE FOUNDATION FOR HIS SON'S FUTURE ACHIEVEMENTS.

BHIMRAO WENT AGAIN TO SHRI KELUSKAR FOR GUIDANCE.
I SUGGEST YOU SEE THE MAHARAJA OF BARODA. HIS STATE HAS PLANS TO SEND A FEW STUDENTS ABROAD FOR FURTHER STUDIES.

SOON—
I HAVE JUST COME FROM BARODA. I HAVE BEEN SELECTED. BUT I HAD TO SIGN AN AGREEMENT TO SERVE BARODA STATE FOR TEN YEARS ON COMPLETION OF MY STUDIES.

BHIMRAO ARRIVED IN NEW YORK IN JULY 1913.
I FEEL SO FREE HERE. THERE ARE NO SOCIAL RESTRAINTS ON ME. I CAN DO ALMOST ANYTHING I PLEASE.
THE FREEDOM AND EQUALITY IN THE U.S.A. WAS A NOVEL EXPERIENCE FOR BHIMRAO.

HE WORKED ALMOST EIGHTEEN HOURS A DAY.
IN 1915 HE TOOK HIS M.A. DEGREE AND GOT HIS PH.D. THE NEXT YEAR.

HAVING COMPLETED HIS STUDIES IN THE U.S.A. IN LESS THAN THE STIPULATED TIME, HE PROCEEDED TO LONDON.
I MUST HAVE A DEGREE IN LAW AND I MUST UNDERTAKE FURTHER STUDIES IN ECONOMICS.

BUT AMBEDKAR WAS RECALLED TO INDIA BY THE DEWAN OF BARODA. WHEN HE ARRIVED AT BARODA, NO GOVERNMENT OFFICIAL RECEIVED HIM AT THE STATION.
BARODA

HE WENT FROM HOTEL TO HOTEL, LOOKING FOR A ROOM. BUT NO ONE WOULD TAKE HIM IN.
YOU ARE THE NEW OFFICER, AREN'T YOU? SORRY, WE HAVE NO ROOMS FOR UNTOUCH-ABLES.
AT LAST HE FOUND ACCOMMO-DATION IN A PARSI GUEST HOUSE, BUT IT WAS ONLY BECAUSE HE TOOK CARE TO KEEP HIS IDENTITY A SECRET.

WHEN HE ENTERED HIS OFFICE THE NEXT DAY, THE PEON ROLLED UP THE CARPET LEST IT SHOULD BE POLLUTED.

HE WAS GIVEN A TABLE IN A CORNER. THE PEON WOULD NOT GO NEAR HIM EVEN TO HAND OVER FILES.
TAKE THIS FILE!

WHEN THE PARSIS IN THE GUEST HOUSE CAME TO KNOW OF HIS IDENTITY—
WHO ARE YOU?
I AM A HINDU.

YOU ARE NOT. YOU ARE A DESPICABLE UNTOUCHABLE.
GET OUT!

I'LL GO, BUT PLEASE GIVE ME SOME TIME.
WE WON'T GIVE YOU A SECOND! LEAVE AT ONCE!

AMBEDKAR WAS THROWN OUT. NO ONE IN THE CITY WOULD GIVE HIM SHELTER.
I DON'T HAVE TO STAY IN A PLACE WHERE I AM NOT RESPECTED.

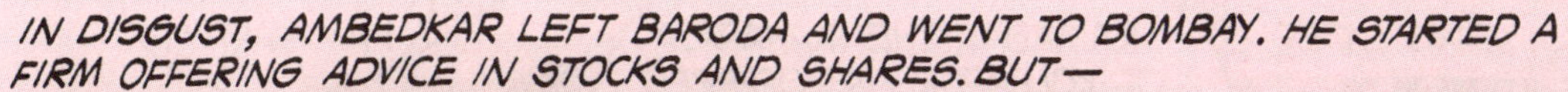
IN DISGUST, AMBEDKAR LEFT BARODA AND WENT TO BOMBAY. HE STARTED A FIRM OFFERING ADVICE IN STOCKS AND SHARES. BUT—

ARE YOU CONSULTING AMBEDKAR?
YES, HE IS AN EXPERT.

DON'T YOU KNOW HE IS AN UNTOUCHABLE?
UNTOUCHABLE! I WON'T GO TO HIM HEREAFTER.
SO AMBEDKAR HAD TO CLOSE DOWN HIS FIRM.

HE SECURED A JOB AS LECTURER IN SYDENHAM COLLEGE IN NOVEMBER 1918.
HE IS THE BEST TEACHER IN THIS COLLEGE.
YES. HE IS A BRILLIANT SCHOLAR.

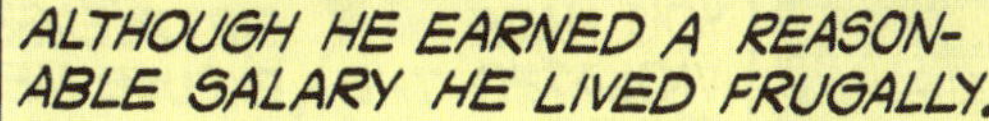
ALTHOUGH HE EARNED A REASON-ABLE SALARY HE LIVED FRUGALLY.

I'M SORRY. I CAN'T SPARE MORE FOR THE HOUSEHOLD EXPENSES. I WANT TO SAVE MONEY TO GO TO LONDON TO CONTINUE MY STUDIES.
DON'T WORRY. I'LL MANAGE.

PIOUS RAMABAI SAW TO IT THAT AMBEDKAR WAS NOT DISTURBED.
NO, I WON'T TELL HIM THAT LITTLE YASHWANT IS ILL. LET HIM STUDY IN PEACE.

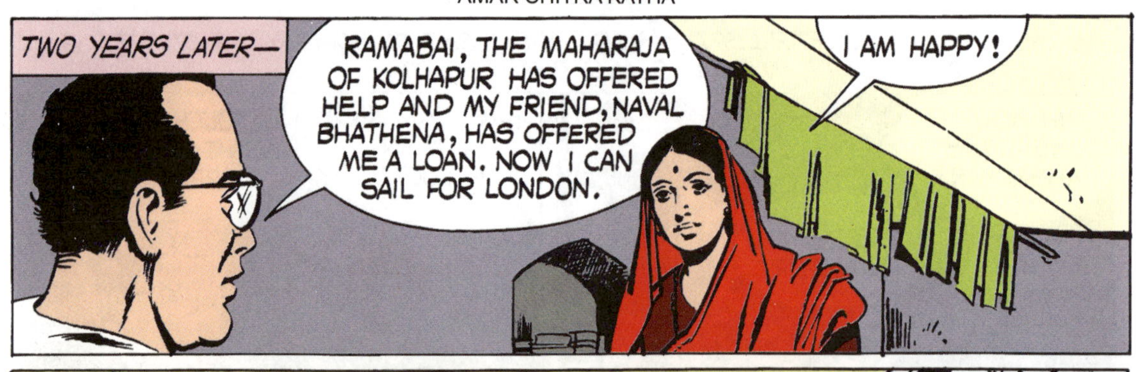

IN LONDON, AMBEDKAR RESUMED HIS STUDIES IN ECONOMICS AND ALSO KEPT TERMS FOR THE BAR AT GRAY'S INN. HE DID NOT HAVE ENOUGH MONEY TO BUY ALL THE BOOKS HE NEEDED.

I MUST STUDY FROM MORNING TILL EVENING AT THE BRITISH MUSEUM LIBRARY.

I SEE YOU READING EVERY DAY FROM MORNING TO EVENING. WHY DON'T YOU TAKE A BREAK FOR LUNCH LIKE EVERYBODY ELSE?
SIR, I CAN'T AFFORD TO HAVE LUNCH OUT-SIDE. I SAVE ONE SANDWICH FROM MY BREAKFAST AND EAT IT AT NOON WITH A GLASS OF WATER.

THE LIBRARIAN WAS MOVED TO LEARN OF THE SAD PLIGHT OF THIS YOUNG STUDENT WHO WAS DISCIPLINED AND DEVOTED TO LEARNING.
ALL RIGHT! I WILL SPARE YOU THIS TIME BUT ON THE CONDITION THAT FROM NOW ON YOU WILL JOIN ME FOR LUNCH IN MY ROOM.
DR. AMBEDKAR GRATEFULLY ACCEPTED THE ENGLISHMAN'S OFFER.

IN 1923, HE RETURNED TO INDIA, QUALIFIED AS A BARRISTER AND A SCHOLAR IN ECONOMICS. BUT—
MY QUALIFICATIONS MEAN NOTHING. UNTOUCHABILITY IS AN OBSTACLE EVEN IN MY PROFESSIONAL PRACTICE. I MUST WORK FOR THE UPLIFT OF MY COMMUNITY.

SOME TIME LATER A GOVERNMENT DIRECTIVE ANNOUNCED THAT NO INSTITUTION AIDED BY PUBLIC FUNDS COULD REFUSE ADMISSION TO UNTOUCHABLES.
THIS IS ALL THE WORK OF THAT UNTOUCHABLE —AMBEDKAR.
WHY BLAME HIM WHEN ONE OF OUR OWN MEN, S. K. BOLE, MOVED THE BILL?

AMBEDKAR FOUNDED AN ASSOCIATION CALLED BAHISHKRIT HITAKARINI SABHA AND UNDER ITS AUSPICES STARTED HOSTELS, SCHOOLS AND FREE LIBRARIES. ONE DAY—
CONGRATULATIONS ON YOUR NOMINATION TO THE BOMBAY LEGISLATIVE COUNCIL! I KNOW YOU WILL DO GOOD WORK.
I WILL DO EVERYTHING I CAN TO IMPROVE THE LOT OF THE UNTOUCHABLES.

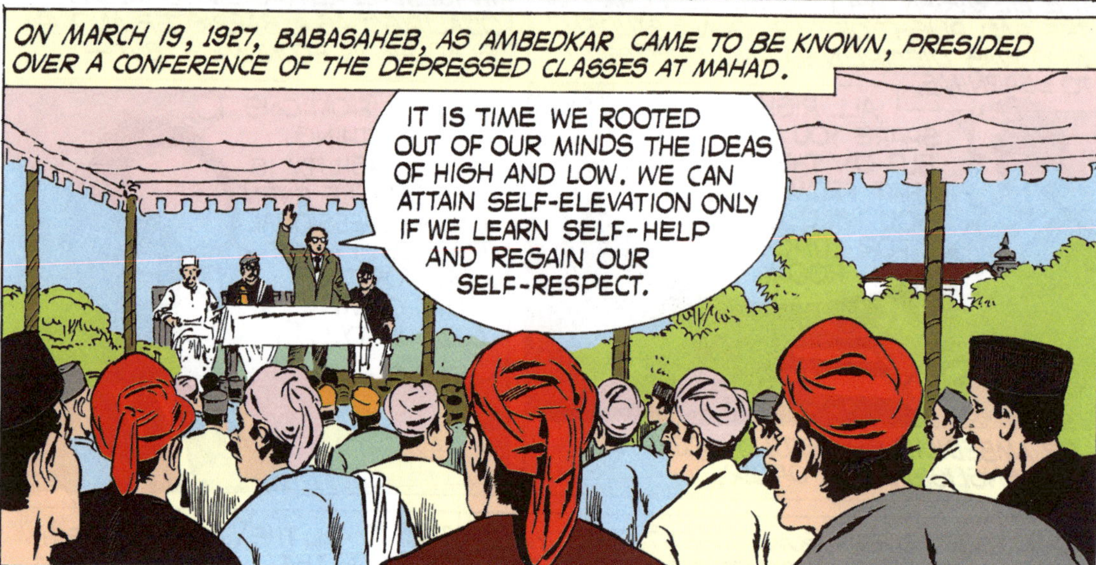
ON MARCH 19, 1927, BABASAHEB, AS AMBEDKAR CAME TO BE KNOWN, PRESIDED OVER A CONFERENCE OF THE DEPRESSED CLASSES AT MAHAD.
IT IS TIME WE ROOTED OUT OF OUR MINDS THE IDEAS OF HIGH AND LOW. WE CAN ATTAIN SELF-ELEVATION ONLY IF WE LEARN SELF-HELP AND REGAIN OUR SELF-RESPECT.

LIBERTY IS NEVER GIFTED AWAY; IT HAS TO BE FOUGHT FOR. THE MAHAD MUNICIPALITY THREW OPEN THE TANK FOUR YEARS AGO. BUT SO FAR NOT ONE OF US HAS DRAWN WATER FROM THE TANK. TODAY WE SHALL.

AMBEDKAR LED HIS MEN TO THE CHOWDAR TANK.
DRAW WATER FROM THE TANK? DO WE DARE DO THAT?
LET'S SEE WHAT BABASAHEB WILL DO.

AT THE TANK, AMBEDKAR TOOK SOME WATER IN HIS CUPPED HANDS...

...AND DRANK IT.
HE HAS DONE IT.

THE GESTURE HAD A REMARKABLE EFFECT. AMBEDKAR HAD EXORCIZED FEAR FROM THE MINDS OF HIS PEOPLE. THOUSANDS OF THEM DRANK WATER FROM THE PUBLIC TANK AND MADE HISTORY.

AFTER THEY HAD DISPERSED, SOME CASTE HINDUS HAD A MEETING.
OUR TANK HAS BEEN POLLUTED!
THOSE PEOPLE MUST BE TAUGHT A LESSON.

ARMED WITH STONES, THE CASTE HINDUS WENT TO THE VENUE OF THE CONFERENCE. MANY DELEGATES HAD ALREADY LEFT AND MANY OTHERS WERE PREPARING TO LEAVE.

BEAT THEM!
DON'T SPARE ANYONE!

WHEN HIS PEOPLE LATER APPEALED TO AMBEDKAR —
VIOLENCE HAS BEEN LET LOOSE!
GIVE US THE WORD, SIR, AND WE SHALL FINISH THEM.
NO, VIOLENCE WILL NOT HELP. WE'LL DO NOTHING UNLAWFUL. I HAVE GIVEN MY WORD THAT WE WILL AGITATE PEACEFULLY.
AMBEDKAR HAD PROMISED THE POLICE THAT HE WOULD KEEP HIS PEOPLE UNDER CONTROL. THUS HE PREVENTED A BLOOD BATH.

IN THE PAGES OF HIS NEWLY STARTED JOURNAL, BAHISHKRIT BHARAT, HE EXHORTED HIS PEOPLE TO ENTER THE KALA RAM TEMPLE AT NASIK. ON MARCH 3, 1930, HIS FOLLOWERS WENT ON SATYAGRAHA AT THE ENTRANCE OF THE TEMPLE.

THE SATYAGRAHA CONTINUED FOR A MONTH, TILL THE EVE OF THE ANNUAL PROCESSION OF THE TEMPLE CHARIOT—

ALL RIGHT, LET THE STRONG MEN FROM BOTH THE SIDES DRAW THE CHARIOT.

IN THAT CASE WE SHALL CALL OFF THE SATYAGRAHA.

BUT AMBEDKAR'S MEN WERE DECEIVED BECAUSE THE CHARIOT WAS PUSHED PAST THEM AT GREAT SPEED.

THEY ARE PELTING US WITH STONES.

LET THEM DO SO. WE SHALL REMAIN FIRM.

AMBEDKAR'S FOLLOWERS CONTINUED TO AGITATE AND THE TEMPLE REMAINED CLOSED FOR ABOUT A YEAR.

MEANWHILE THE FREEDOM MOVEMENT HAD GAINED MOMENTUM UNDER THE LEADERSHIP OF MAHATMA GANDHI. IN 1930, A ROUND TABLE CONFERENCE WAS HELD BY THE BRITISH GOVERNMENT IN LONDON TO FRAME A CONSTITUTION FOR INDIA. AMBEDKAR REPRESENTED THE DEPRESSED CLASSES.

THE DEPRESSED CLASSES OF INDIA ALSO JOIN IN THE DEMAND FOR REPLACING THE BRITISH GOVERNMENT BY A GOVERNMENT OF THE PEOPLE AND BY THE PEOPLE.... OUR WRONGS HAVE REMAINED AS OPEN SORES AND THEY HAVE NOT BEEN RIGHTED ALTHOUGH 150 YEARS OF BRITISH RULE HAVE ROLLED AWAY. OF WHAT GOOD IS SUCH A GOVERNMENT TO ANYBODY?

SOON AFTERWARDS, A SECOND ROUND TABLE CONFERENCE WAS CALLED. MAHATMA GANDHI WHO HAD BOYCOTTED THE FIRST CONFERENCE AGREED TO REPRESENT THE CONGRESS PARTY. BEFORE PROCEEDING FOR LONDON, AT GANDHI'S REQUEST, AMBEDKAR VISITED HIM AT MANI BHUVAN IN BOMBAY.

FROM THE REPORTS THAT HAVE REACHED ME OF YOUR SPEECHES AT THE FIRST ROUND TABLE CONFERENCE I KNOW YOU ARE A PATRIOT OF STERLING WORTH.

AT THE SECOND ROUND TABLE CONFERENCE IN LONDON —
I ASK FOR A SEPARATE ELECTORATE FOR THE DEPRESSED CLASSES OF INDIA. HINDUISM HAS GIVEN US ONLY INSULTS, MISERY AND HUMILIATION.

THE CONFERENCE ENDED IN A STALEMATE. BUT AMBEDKAR WAS LIONISED ON HIS RETURN TO BOMBAY BECAUSE HE HAD BROUGHT THE PLIGHT OF THE UNTOUCHABLES TO THE ATTENTION OF THE WORLD.
AMBEDKAR KI JAI!
I APPEAL TO YOU NOT TO IDOLISE ME.
AMBEDKAR'S WIFE WAS DEEPLY RELIGIOUS.
LET'S GO TO PANDHARPUR. I'VE BEEN LONGING TO BEHOLD LORD VITHOBA.
BUT WE WON'T BE ALLOWED TO ENTER THE TEMPLE, RAMABAI.
IT DOESN'T MATTER. WE WILL STAND AT THE ENTRANCE AND BEHOLD THE LORD.
NO. I DON'T LIKE THE IDEA.
BUT HE CONSOLED HIS WIFE.
WHY BOTHER ABOUT PANDHARPUR, WHERE WE ARE KEPT AT A DISTANCE EVEN FROM THE IMAGE OF GOD? BY OUR OWN VIRTUOUS LIFE, SELFLESS SERVICE AND SPOTLESS SACRIFICE IN THE CAUSE OF DOWN-TRODDEN HUMANITY, WE WILL CREATE ANOTHER PANDHARPUR!

HIS HOUSE HAD INDEED BECOME A PANDHARPUR FOR THE UNTOUCHABLES, WHO LOOKED UPON AMBEDKAR AS THEIR LIBERATOR.
BABASAHEB, THE GOVERNMENT HAS AWARDED SEPARATE ELECTORATES FOR US.
GOOD, WE HAVE WON THE FIRST ROUND.

BUT GANDHIJI WAS OPPOSED TO THE DIVISION OF ELECTORATES ON THE BASIS OF CASTE. TO PROTEST, GANDHIJI, WHO WAS IN THE YERAVDA JAIL AT THE TIME, BEGAN A FAST. AT A MEETING OF NATIONAL LEADERS IN BOMBAY—
DR. AMBEDKAR, YOU ALONE CAN SAVE GANDHI'S LIFE. PLEASE AGREE TO HIS PLEA.

AMBEDKAR EXPLAINED HIS STAND.
I SHALL NOT BETRAY THE JUST AND LEGITIMATE INTERESTS OF MY PEOPLE, EVEN IF YOU HANG ME FROM THE NEAREST LAMP POST.

LATER HE VISITED GANDHIJI AT THE YERAVDA JAIL.
WE MUST BE ONE AND INDIVISIBLE. GIVE HINDUISM A LAST CHANCE TO MAKE A VOLUNTARY EXPIATION FOR ITS SINFUL PAST.
I WILL THINK IT OVER.

NO SOLUTION SEEMED POSSIBLE. AT LAST, AMBEDKAR AGREED TO SIGN THE POONA PACT, UNDER WHICH, INSTEAD OF SEPARATE ELECTORATES, MORE REPRESENTATION WAS TO BE GIVEN TO THE DEPRESSED CLASSES.
THE DIVISION OF THE PEOPLE ON CASTE LINES HAS BEEN AVERTED.

THOUGH POLITICALLY ACTIVE, HE ALWAYS REMAINED A SCHOLAR FIRST. HE HAD AMASSED A UNIQUE LIBRARY OF OVER 50,000 BOOKS FOR WHICH HE BUILT A SUITABLE HOUSE AT DADAR* AND NAMED IT RAJAGRIHA.

IN MAY 1935, A PERSONAL TRAGEDY BEFELL AMBEDKAR. HIS BELOVED WIFE, RAMABAI, DIED.

MEANWHILE, THE POONA PACT REMAINED A MERE DOCUMENT. AMBEDKAR WAS UNHAPPY. AT A CONFERENCE OF UNTOUCHABLES, HELD IN YEOLA—
WE HAVE NOT BEEN ABLE TO SECURE THE BAREST OF HUMAN RIGHTS .... I AM BORN A HINDU. I COULDN'T HELP IT. BUT I SOLEMNLY ASSURE YOU THAT I WILL NOT DIE A HINDU.

* IN NORTH BOMBAY

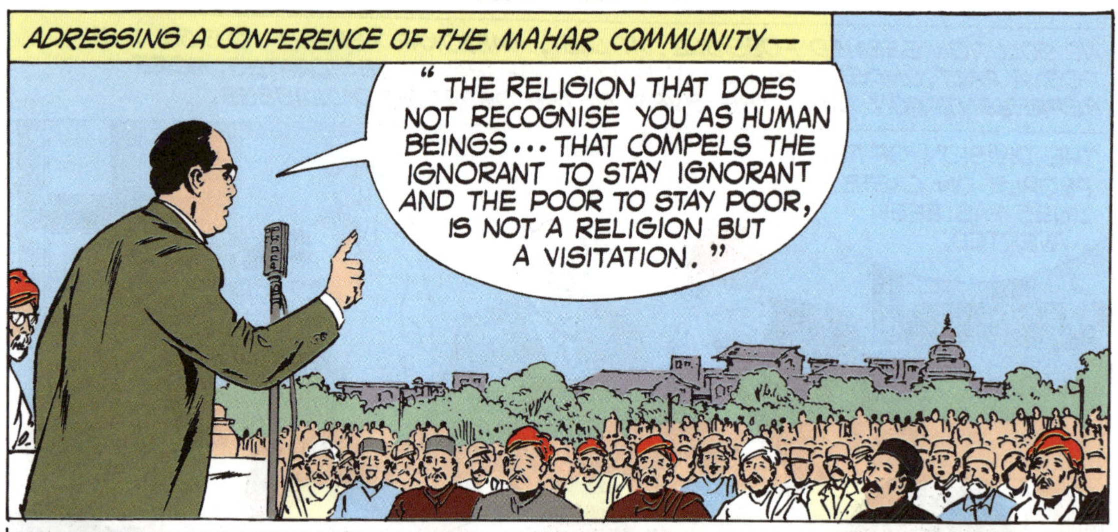
ADRESSING A CONFERENCE OF THE MAHAR COMMUNITY—
"THE RELIGION THAT DOES NOT RECOGNISE YOU AS HUMAN BEINGS... THAT COMPELS THE IGNORANT TO STAY IGNORANT AND THE POOR TO STAY POOR, IS NOT A RELIGION BUT A VISITATION."

THE FIRST ELECTIONS, UNDER THE 1935 GOVERNMENT OF INDIA ACT, BEGAN.
I APPEAL TO YOU IN THE NAME OF OUR NEW PARTY— THE INDEPENDENT LABOUR PARTY.
AMBEDKAR AND FOURTEEN OTHERS OF THE INDEPENDENT LABOUR PARTY WERE ELECTED TO THE BOMBAY LEGISLATIVE ASSEMBLY.

IN 1939, THE SECOND WORLD WAR BROKE OUT. THE CONGRESS MINISTRIES RESIGNED. IN JULY 1942, THE VICEROY APPOINTED AMBEDKAR AS LABOUR MINISTER IN THE EXECUTIVE COUNCIL. AT A RECEPTION, GIVEN IN HIS HONOUR—
I WAS BORN OF THE POOR. I WAS BROUGHT UP AMONG THEM, HAVE LIVED AMONG THEM. I HAVE SLEPT LIKE THEM ON DAMP FLOORS COVERED WITH SACK-CLOTH AND SHARED THE SORROWS OF MY PEOPLE. I WILL REMAIN ABSOLUTELY UNCHANGED IN MY ATTITUDE TO MY FRIENDS AND TO THE REST OF THE WORLD.
HE FORMED THE ALL INDIA SCHEDULED CASTES FEDERATION IN 1942. IN SPITE OF HIS HARD WORK THE FEDERATION FARED BADLY AT THE GENERAL ELECTIONS HELD IN SEPTEMBER 1945.

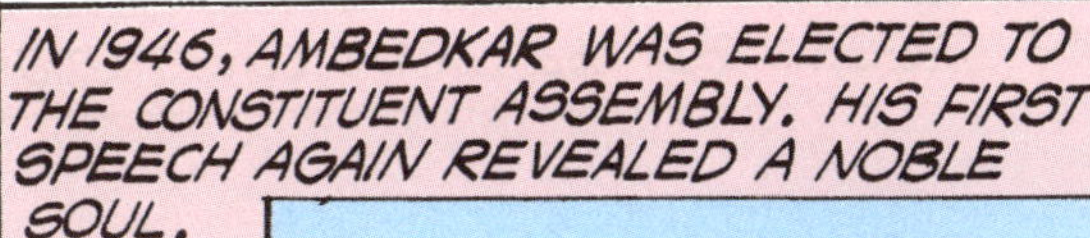
IN 1946, AMBEDKAR WAS ELECTED TO THE CONSTITUENT ASSEMBLY. HIS FIRST SPEECH AGAIN REVEALED A NOBLE SOUL.
...AND WITH ALL OUR CASTES AND CREEDS I HAVE NOT THE SLIGHTEST HESITATION IN SAYING THAT WE SHALL IN SOME FORM BE A UNITED PEOPLE.
THE THIRD SESSION OF THE CONSTITUENT ASSEMBLY ADOPTED A RESOLUTION MAKING UNTOUCHABILITY AN OFFENCE.

WHEN INDIA BECAME INDEPENDENT IN AUGUST 1947, AMBEDKAR BECAME THE FIRST LAW MINISTER OF INDEPENDENT INDIA.
WHAT AN ACHIEVEMENT! THIS GREAT MAN WILL LEAD HIS COMMUNITY TO HONOUR AND DIGNITY.

THE CONSTITUENT ASSEMBLY MADE DR. AMBEDKAR THE CHAIRMAN OF THE COMMITEE APPOINTED TO DRAFT THE CONSTITUTION OF INDIA. AND THE BURDEN OF PREPARING A CONSTITUTION FOR THE WORLD'S LARGEST DEMOCRACY FELL UPON DR. AMBEDKAR.

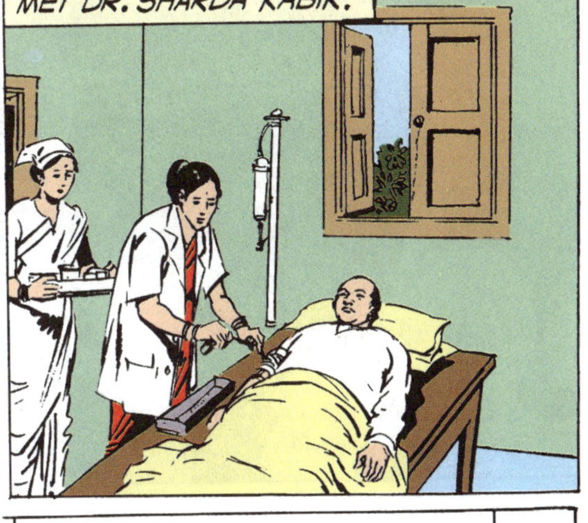
AFTER COMPLETING THE DRAFT CONSTITUTION, AMBEDKAR FELL ILL. AT THE NURSING HOME IN BOMBAY HE MET DR. SHARDA KABIR.

HE MARRIED HER IN APRIL 1948.

ON NOVEMBER 4, 1948, DR AMBEDKAR PRESENTED THE DRAFT CONSTITUTION TO THE CONSTITUENT ASSEMBLY.
...AND I APPEAL TO ALL INDIANS TO BE A NATION BY DISCARDING CASTES WHICH HAVE BROUGHT ABOUT SEPARATION IN SOCIAL LIFE AND CREATED JEALOUSY AND HATRED.
ON NOVEMBER 26, 1949, THE CONSTITUENT ASSEMBLY ADOPTED THE CONSTITUTION IN THE NAME OF THE PEOPLE OF INDIA.

DR. AMBEDKAR WAS INVITED TO THE BUDDHIST CONFERENCE AT CEYLON. ON HIS RETURN HE SPOKE IN BOMBAY AT THE BUDDHA TEMPLE.
IN ORDER TO END THEIR HARDSHIPS, PEOPLE SHOULD EMBRACE BUDDHISM. I AM GOING TO DEVOTE THE REST OF MY LIFE TO THE REVIVAL AND SPREAD OF BUDDHISM IN INDIA.

FOR THE NEXT EIGHT YEARS, DR. AMBEDKAR CARRIED ON A RELENTLESS FIGHT AGAINST SOCIAL EVILS AND SUPERSTITIONS. ON OCTOBER 14, 1956 AT NAGPUR, AMBEDKAR EMBRACED BUDDHISM.

LATER HE INITIATED A VAST CROWD OF FOLLOWERS, NUMBERING OVER THREE LAKHS, INTO BUDDHISM.
BUDDHAM SARANAM GACCHAMI.
BUDDHAM SARANAM GACCHAMI

SEVEN WEEKS LATER ON DECEMBER 6, 1956, AT HIS DELHI RESIDENCE, DR. AMBEDKAR BREATHED HIS LAST. HIS BODY WAS TAKEN TO BOMBAY THE NEXT DAY. A TWO-MILE LONG CROWD THRONGED AT THE FUNERAL. BOMBAY HAD NEVER SEEN SUCH A FUNERAL PROCESSION BEFORE.

AT THE DADAR CEMETERY THAT EVENING, EMINENT LEADERS PAID THEIR LAST TRIBUTES TO BABASAHEB. THE PYRE WAS LIT ACCORDING TO BUDDHIST RITES AND A GREAT SON OF MOTHER INDIA, WHO HAD FOUGHT VALIANTLY FOR HER OPPRESSED CHILDREN, WAS LAID TO REST.

TRIBUTES TO BABASAHEB AMBEDKAR

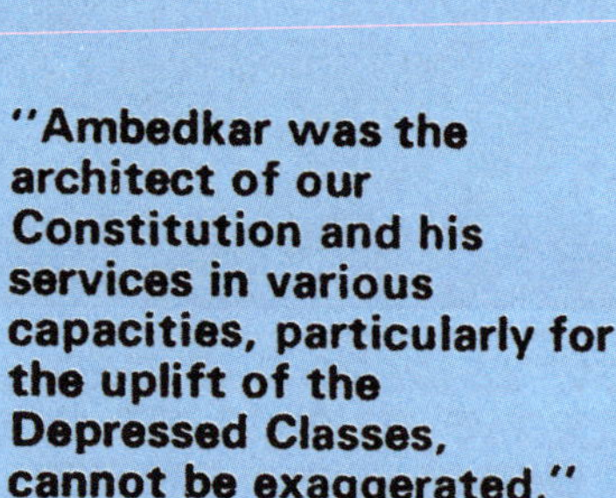

"Ambedkar was the architect of our Constitution and his services in various capacities, particularly for the uplift of the Depressed Classes, cannot be exaggerated."

-Dr. Rajendra Prasad.

"Ambedkar was a thoroughly upright person and a man with a keen jurist sense, a proud and irreconcilable heart, great learning and when approached in right spirit, full of friendliness."

-C. Rajagopalachari.

"Ambedkar was known and honoured throughout the world chiefly as a champion of the untouchables. What is perhaps not so well known is that he put a profound impress upon India's major legal structures."

-The New York Times.

"I imagine that the way he will be remembered most will be as a symbol of the revolt against all the oppressive features of Hindu society. He rebelled against something against which all ought to rebel and we have, in fact, rebelled in various degrees.

I have no doubt, whether we agree with him or not in many matters, that perseverance, that persistance, and that, if I may use the word, sometime virulence of his opposition to all this, did keep the people's mind awake and did not allow them to become complacent about matters which could not be forgotten, and helped in rousing up those groups in our country which had suffered for so long in the past."

-Pandit Jawaharlal Nehru.